Butterscotch Dreams

Pembroke Publishers Limited
528 Hood Road
Markham Ontario L3R 3K9

Canadian Cataloguing in Publication Data

Dunn, Sonja, 1931-
  Butterscotch dreams

Includes index.
ISBN 0-921217-07-2

1. Chants. 2. Music in education. 3. Poetry and children. I. Pamenter, Lou. II. Title.

GV1215.D86 1987   398'.8   C87-093212-8

Published in the U.S.A. by
Heinemann Educational Books, Inc.
361 Hanover St.
Portsmouth, N.H. 03801

Library of Congress Cataloguing-in-Publication Data
Dunn, Sonja.
  Butterscotch dreams / Sonja Dunn.
    p.   cm.
  Includes index.
  ISBN 0-435-08497-6
  1. Choral recitations. I. Title.
PN4305.C4D86   1989
808.5'5--dc19   89-30384
                                                       CIP

Typesetting by Jay Tee Graphics Ltd.

Printed and bound in Canada by Webcom Limited

0 9 8 7

CHANTS FOR FUN AND LEARNING

Butterscotch Dreams

Sonja Dunn

Heinemann

Acknowledgments

I would like to thank my editor and co-author, Lou Pamenter, for her work in the production of this collection of my original chants, and the publishers for their interest. I would also like to thank my family: Bill, Paul, Kevin, Deborah, Lisa, and Brian for their support, and for their sometimes unintentional contributions to my chants. A special thank you to my father, Wolodymyr Serotiuk. The support of my friends at CANSCAIP has been invaluable. As well, I would like to acknowledge the encouragement I have received from the many educators and children with whom I have worked around the world.

The Alvin Schwartz poem that was the inspiration for "Dance of the bones", page 59, was "Aaron Kelly's Bones" from *Scary Stories To Tell In The Dark*, a Lippincott Junior Book. The translation for "Un deux trois", page 32 was done by François Crépeau. "Would you still come home?", page 86, was previously published in *Books Alive, Grade Five*, Doubleday & Company. "Singing sand", page 96, was previously published in *Pingo Expressways II*, "Wonders of the Natural Environment", Gage Publishing Company. "The clown," page 21, was previously published in *Impressions Big Book Kindergarden 1*, Holt, Rinehart & Winston Canada.

The music for "The blanket doesn't feel right" was adapted from a traditional folksong but the words are mine. The words and music for "A story for You", "Goodbye," and "It's so easy to say hello" are mine. Thanks to Thom McKercher and Ron Forrester for the transcription of the music.

I would like to acknowledge the help given by Barbara Stubley in clarifying the directions for making a story skirt.

John Zehethofer must be thanked for his attractive book design and David Prothero for his delightful illustrations.

Contents

Introduction

Take a chance
on a chant
It's a whole
lot of fun
You can shriek
You can pant
Make your voices like one
You can say
all the words
in a rhythmical way
You can cheer
loud and clear
with a Hip! Hip! Hooray!

A chant is a group of words that come alive when given a rhythmical reading. That rhythm can be the traditional sing-song, measured reading, or with a change in inflection, in the way words are accented, it can be a talking-blues reading. The rhythm used can make a chant into a cheer. Add simple, supplementary music and a chant becomes a song. A chant is a sound poem with many rhythmical possibilities.

A need for the following collection of chants grew out of the hundreds of practical workshops that I have conducted for educators and children. The energy and stimulation that a chant workshop generates showed that there should be a resource collection available for use by teachers, by parents, by anyone who spends time with children.

I have always been intrigued by the way in which certain words are held together in a rhythmical pattern. I can still remember the pleasure of learning — by rote — the words of Wilfred Campbell's "Indian Summer" in elementary school. The words still surface when the leaves start to change color:

> Along the line of smoky hills
> The crimson forest stands
> And all the day the blue-jay calls
> Throughout the autumn lands.

I can also remember the playground chant:

> Liar, liar
> Ten feet higher
> Caught his pants
> On a telephone wire.

Perhaps the inherent rhythm of poems like Campbell's and playground chants like "Liar, liar" have been the catalyst for the sixty chants I have developed for this collection — the aesthetic and the absurd.

There are many ways to introduce chanting to children. Chanting can be introduced one-on-one or to a large group. Chanting does not require musical talent, ability to play an instrument, or singing lessons. The simplest way to introduce a chant is by rote. For example, "Take a chance on a chant" can be chanted be one person several times. Then individual children or groups of four could chant single lines. Establish a rhythm, point to each child or group at the appropriate time, keeping the beat steady. The last line can be chanted or shouted by everyone.

It is a good idea to let children see the words; an overhead projector can be used with children who have developed some reading skills. Once children realize that a chant is any group of words with a beat, they will learn to recognize the sing-song possibilities of other chants.

Throughout the book I have given suggestions for the introduction of specific chants, but, basically, any chant can be introduced by one person reading it aloud several times, and then encouraging others to join in. A chant can be enjoyed by one, two, or any number.

Don't be alarmed that the chants do not always follow the rules of punctuation. Children are encouraged to find their own rhythm for a chant, and providing all the punctuation might be limiting. Sometimes a hint about a possible rhythm is given by the spacing of lines or by the use of capitalization.

I have organized the chants under such topics as Friends, Work, Food, and Geography. The chants do not have to be used within these categories; they simply provide the vehicle for springboard learning activities. Chants are successful with children because they enjoy doing them, but they are open-ended pieces that allow for the development of many skills.

Any speech exercise based on a strong rhythm contributes to the development of speech and language skills. Language learning is accelerated by having fun with and exploring the rhythm in words. An energetic approach, using oral repetition with rhythmical expression, leads to pleasant, stimulating experiences. As soon as children begin to verbalize, they become fascinated with the possibilities and structures of words and phrases. They love natural repetition, and changing the sounds of words. Chanting should provoke a need to explore a variety of other words, phrases, rhymes, and rhythms. Children with speech problems can be helped with the device of a chant.

Chanting, with its rhythmical repetition of words, transcends language differences. It is useful for children in programs of English as a second language and English as a dialect, and for beginning readers. Speaking and listening comprehension skills are improved by the highly motivating and appealing rhymes of chants. One class of Grade 7 and 8 children, learning English as a second dialect, became able to group words into phrases from having fun with chants.

Drama can be a link between speech and writing. Through drama, children are guided to imagine, explore, enact, communicate, and reflect on ideas, concepts, and feelings. Since most chants can be developed dramatically, they encourage all the wonderful skills possible from drama.

Body movement added to a chant allows for an integrated approach, using eyes, ears, voices, emotions, and group work. Movement and role-playing that use action and dialogue can lead to intellectual, physical, and emotional growth. A chant almost always has the potential for simple actions, and most chants can be vehicles for more involved actions.

Simple actions can enhance the awareness of rhythm: finger-snapping, thigh-slapping, head-bobbing, clapping, jumping, and crouching. Once the awareness of rhythm is increased, children's dexterity in accompanying movements seems to improve; motor skills and eye/hand co-ordination improve.

Talking blues chanting often encourages the addition of a great deal of body movement:

>Do you like to breakdance on the street?
>Right on!
>Do you show off to the guys you meet?
>Right on!
>Do you do the moonwalk on the beat?
>Right on!
>Do you keep the rhythm nice and neat?
>Right on!
>Do you spin your body off your feet?
>Right on!
>Do you use your head to make a seat?
>Right on!
>Breakdancer, breakdancer, you are sweet.
>Let's dance!

The rhythm of a chant can be emphasized by using simple instruments. Make your own band. The music in the background of a chant establishes the beat. Cowbells, sticks, tambourines, shakers, triangles, drums are all effective beat-reinforcers. A very simple melody can be added to some chants to make a song. The tune for the following "Story" chant is a simple one. This chant acknowledges that storytelling is a personal way to touch children — and all chants have a storytelling aspect.

>A story, a story for You
>A story for Kevin and Sue
>A story to cheer you
>while sitting right near you
>a story, a story for you
>
>A story about the three bears
>of Goldilocks going upstairs

of witches and places and feelings and fun
A story to tell to someone

Some chanting for Vancy and Sean
for Ahmed and Deborah and Ron
Some chanting for Lisa and Brian and Paul
Some chanting and stories for all!

A stor-y, a stor-y for you A
stor-y for Kev-in and Sue A
stor-y to cheer you while sit-ting right near you a
stor-y a stor-y for you

Music, dance, poetry, and painting all use elements of rhythm, color, and line to express feelings and ideas. Chanting can be a springboard into all the arts.

In my workshops, I have discovered that a simple chant can lead to improved listening skills, to better control of oral language, to increased reading ability, to stronger ordering or sequencing skills, to the development of physical co-ordination and social skills. I have found that children can be inventive and expressive when they chant. But they also have fun — and so do I!

Participation is the key. Chanting is not a passive activity. So, please, don't just read the chants in this collection. Do them!

Sonja Dunn

Actions, Rhymes, and Mimes

Chants are fun! I know — because I have watched children of all ages smiling and laughing when they are introduced to chants. Children are "caught up" in the rhythm of a chant. They play with words, they enjoy the rhymes, they role play, mime, and find all kinds of movements to suit the tempo.

Cleano

We wash our hands
with a rub rub rub
We take a bath
with a scrub scrub scrub
We take a swim
with a glub glub glub
Rub rub rub
Scrub scrub scrub
Glub glub glub
Cleano cleano
Rub scrub glub

This chant illustrates the co-ordination of actions and rhymes. The repetition of the rhymes creates a rhythm within the chant. Rhythmical speech encourages fluency in speech. I have watched both hearing-impaired children and children with speech difficulties gain greater fluency from listening to and repeating chants.

Chant "Cleano" several times in unison. Let the children add the simple actions that are suggested by the words. New words and mimetics can be given by the children. They'll think of things they love — and things they hate: washing dishes, making beds, eating, skating . . .

When simple actions are added, children are exercising, stretching their bodies — without even being aware of it.

The rhythm of the chant can be emphasized by letting some of the chanters become musicians. Try handmade shakers, clickers, or beaters, triangles or bells as accompanying instruments. The reinforcement of the beat by the musicians encourages a greater rhythmical sense. Or, as I say to a group, "Do you feel the beat?"

Husha

Husha husha husha
baby's sleeping
Husha husha husha
momma's leaping
Husha husha husha
daddy's sweeping
Husha husha husha
sister's creeping
Husha husha husha
brother's weeping
Husha husha husha
Sh Sh Sh

The rhythm of this chant can be strengthened by having one half of the group repeat "sh" while the other half chants. Then ask them to switch parts. All the action words can be acted out.

Someone's singing

Someone's singing
      Tra la la
Someone's calling
      Ma ma ma
Someone's laughing
      Ha ha ha
Someone's cheering
      Rah rah rah
Someone's dancing
      Cha cha cha
Someone's talking
      Blah blah blah
Someone's teasing
      Nya nya nya
Someone's sleeping
      Sh sh sh

Each action has a sound to go with it. The chant can be done in unison, or you can ask individuals to chant single lines. New actions and appropriate sounds can be added.

Some of the actions demonstrate emotions. Ask the children to think about what 'laughter' looks like. This can lead to some small-scale role-playing. Little plays that tell the story of a particular emotion can be developed; for instance, a story about happiness, anger, anxiety.

Depending on their maturity, the children might talk about how to handle situations that involve emotions. Such discussions could encompass self-awareness, self-concept, and relationships with others.

Introduce the familiar South African song "Kumbaya" and let the children explore a different rhythm for similar words.

Sunshine cake

You are eating
a sunshine cake

You are gardening
with a rake

You are tasting
a sour grape

You are wearing
a prince's cape

You are wiggling
like a germ

You are holding
a slimy worm

You are climbing
a big steep hill

You are wiping
up a spill

You are flying
like a bat

You are snoozing
like a cat

M ime is the refinement of simple actions; it is a way in which the body can show pictures. "Sunshine cake" is a perfect chant for mime. It may be chanted in unison or some children can be the chorus, chanting, while others mime the actions of the chant.

Individually, or in groups, children can add verses of their own. New verses can be mimed to see if the actual words can be guessed from the actions shown in mime. Drama, in which mime may play a part, often provides a link between speech and writing.

I woke up in the morning

I woke up in the morning
and I jumped out of bed
put some clothes on my body
and a hat on my head
took a leap to the kitchen
and I ate my toast
listened to the news
from coast to coast
looked out the window
to check the sun
ran out the door
to have some fun

This is an action chant too, but one that can be done in different tempos. Let the whole group explore the words and discover a suitable rhythm. The chant can be done with a traditional pattern or it can use the more contemporary ''rap'' pattern. Rap is the chanting that sometimes accompanies break dancing, and requires a more insistent beat.

Different actions will help to define the division of beats, or the metre. I often emphasize a stronger beat by clapping harder or by crouching down low.

Once children discover that a chant can be done in various tempos — fast, slow, and with some of each — discussion can follow about tempo. Ask the children to think about things that move quickly, like a jet; about things that move slowly, like a spider. Something in between might be a skateboard. They can draw pictures of these things. They can imitate the tempos of these things by jumping, running quickly, walking slowly, hopping, reaching high, or crawling.

Parade

I am fun
I am noise and shouting
I am music and high stepping
I am swirling, twirling batons
I am bass and treble sounds
I am spirits soaring high
I am tumbling clowns
I am laughter
I am giants from wonderland
I am shrieks
I am witches from witchland
I am a grand surprise
I am floating fantasy
I am dancing jugglers
I am shivering legs
I am running noses
I am freezing toeses
I am eight reindeer
I am joy and love
bundled in
a fur-trimmed
red suit.

A Santa Claus parade was the obvious inspiration for this
poem, but you can drop the ending or make another if
you want.

Actions and sounds can be added at the end of each line. Ask
the children to think about sounds; about the sounds animals
make, or a water fountain, a pencil sharpener, chalk on
chalkboard, a typewriter. a food blender, an electric razor.

When I start this chant, I might say "I am fun" and follow
with 'Great Fun!' Then, "I am noise and shouting" followed
by 'Yahoo!' "I am music and high stepping" could have a fan-
fare such as 'Ta, Tah, Ta, Tah!' after it. Swirling, twirling batons
could be mimed. "Bass and treble sounds" could be shown as
a low, floor-sweeping gesture followed by a stretch to the sky.
"Spirits soaring high" are, logically, a great leap in the air. Taking
giant steps, laughing, and shrieking like witches come from suc-
cessive lines. What a wonderful parade a group can have!

Let everyone make up a chant that incorporates some of the
sounds the children thought of earlier.

Since "Parade" really is the story of a parade, make up other
dramatic presentations that have words, actions, and sounds to
tell a story.

Drawings, collages, and other visual arts presentations can
allow children to depict parades they have seen.

A circus can generate the same kind of energy as a parade:

> All the crowds
> for miles around
> came to the circus
> to see the clown
> They heard him sing
> They watched him dance
> They laughed and laughed
> At his baggy pants

When I was skinny, I hardly ever thought about food. Now that I am not-so-skinny, I find that I think about food a lot. But I also find that kids, skinny or not, love to talk about food. They'll talk about what they love to eat and what they hate to eat.

Cheers for flavors

We got a C
We got an H
We got an E-R-R-Y
We got a CHERRY CHERRY CHERRY pie.
Cherries are red
Cherries are sweet
Cherry pies are good to eat.

All those years I spent as a cheerleader at Mimico High School in suburban Toronto during the late '40s have finally paid off! Many chants can be treated as cheers, great ice-breakers in any group.

Before beginning a chant such as "Cheers For Flavors", I ask the children to yell out their favorite flavors. Pick one and make it into a simple cheer, using the call-and-response technique. For example:

Give me an L	L
Give me an E	E
Give me a M	M
Give me an O	O
Give me an N	N
What does that spell?	Lemon, lemon, lemon!

The simple call-and-response can always be concluded with a cheer that shouts out the completed word.

The flavor game can be played by letting guesses be made about the identity of the flavor as it is being spelled. Grape, vanilla, strawberry might be flavors to use in this way.

The Cherry Pie chant can be shown on an overhead projector or you can say it aloud several times. It does not take very many repetitions until the children "chime in". Then the chant can be done in unison.

Work out chants for other flavors, using the same measure. Children can choose their 'very favorite' and write a chant for it. For example:

Chocolate
Chocolate
It tastes swell
Chocolate, chocolate
chocolate sweet
That's the stuff I love to eat.

Cheers can be developed for other subjects. Animals, colors, plants, names of people in the group, numbers, place names are only a few of the possible extensions. The yelling-out that is basic to cheers is a good warm-up for any chant.

Butterscotch dreams

Butterscotch butterscotch
Butterscotch pie
For butterscotch flavor
I gladly would die
I love it in cookies
I love it in cake
I crave it in candy
or fudge that I make
It's heaven in sauces
divine in ice-cream
I have butterscotch butterscotch butterscotch
   dreams

So three cheers for butterscotch
   Hip! Hip! Hooray!
It's butterscotch butterscotch
leading the way.

   You might choose vanilla
   and orange sun-kissed
   or settle for chocolate
   at the top of the list
   or vote for banana
   or cheer for pecan
   or strawberry ripple
   but these I would pan.
'Cause I love the flavor
of BUTTERSCOTCH PIE!
For butterscotch butterscotch
I surely would die!

   Ah! Ah! Ah!
   Butterscotch.

I canvassed hundreds of people for a title for this collection of chants — I would ask at workshops, I queried friends, I debated with family members. Most people expressed a real affinity for the word "butterscotch" — it appealed to all the senses. So, "Butterscotch dreams" became the title of the book. And, based on the number of words or images evoked by the word "butterscotch" in my informal polls, I know that children will respond easily to this chant.

Introduce the chant by being a teacher-in-role. Pretend to be the owner of an ice cream parlor or the president of a candy factory. The children are the shareholders. Up until now, the business has been making money; but now, sales for butterscotch are way down and you are facing bankruptcy. The children in the role of shareholders have to find ways to boost the sales of butterscotch.

Maybe a radio commercial is needed to increase interest in the butterscotch flavor. Ask the children for words that could be used to promote sales of butterscotch. Write down all suggestions. Write down the word 'butterscotch' and shout out its letters in unison.

Show the chant on an overhead projector and let everyone chant it. Individuals can be given single words or single lines. During several repetitions of the chant, the sound can be varied from whispers to shouts. Lines such as "You might choose vanilla" can be replaced by snapping fingers to create a new sound. Children can form a cheerleading line that performs some action at every mention of 'butterscotch'. And certainly they can cheer and clap when they reach "Hip! Hip! Hooray!". The final line of "Ah's" can be sung simply, using one or two notes.

Squid sauce

Squid sauce
good for supper
Squid sauce
good for lunch
Squid sauce
good for breakfast
Squid sauce
good for brunch

Catch a little squid
On top of the water
Eat it all up
With bread and butter

T he first time I did this chant, the kids all went 'yuck' and turned up their noses. So, we added 'yuck' as a background chorus during the chant.

Let the children discover an appropriate rhythm. They can play with the words in different ways. The modern rap method, putting emphasis on words that are not as obviously accented, might work. Different cultures present different accenting practices.

"Squid Sauce" is a tongue-twister; it is difficult to do quickly. Let the children speed up the tempo and see how long it is until their tongues twist.

Once the children have found a rhythm they like, they will be able to fit their own food combinations into the same beat.

Junk food

Junk food
Junk food
I love junk food
I eat junk food
I can't stop

Reese's pieces
Greasy French fries
Caramel popcorn
Soda pop

Sticky candy
Gooey choc'late
Salted cheesies
Sugared glop

Junk food
Junk food
I love junk food
I eat junk food
Till I drop!

In any discussion of food, lots of 'junk food' will be mentioned. This chant lets everyone's junk food favorites be included.

After working through the choices given in the chant, ask the children to give their choices. The children can be in a circle and chant their junk food choice in turn. Let them know that if they can't think of one when it is their turn, they can clap to fill in the appropriate rhythm. There is no loss of self-esteem if it is acceptable to fill-in with rhythmical action.

Crackers and crumbs

crackers and crumbs
crackers and crumbs
these are my fingers
these are my thumbs
these are my eyes
these are my ears
they'll all grow big
in the next ten years

A chant can happen anytime, and anywhere. My son Paul and I were having a snack of cheese and crackers while driving in the car. Very soon there were crumbs all over the car, and us. Exclaiming, the way mothers do, I said, ''Cracker crumbs everywhere''. Paul replied in a teasing voice, ''Crackers and crumbs, crackers and crumbs''. The rest was easy. We played with the words until ''Crackers and crumbs'' worked itself into this co-operatively-written chant.

Simple actions make this chant very involving whether done with one child or with many. Fingers, thumbs, eyes, and ears can be shown at the appropriate line. A great leap into the air demonstrates the growing in the last two lines. In a group situation, several children can be given a line to chant and act out together.

As in most chants, finger-snapping, foot-stamping, and clapping can be added to establish the beat. Several people can be a chorus, chanting 'crackers and crumbs' in the background while others do the complete chant.

Un deux trois

Un deux trois
La soupe pour le roi
Quatre cinq six
Mais il veux des saucisses

Un deux trois
Il manque des pois
Sept huit neuf
Le roi aura du boeuf

One two . . . three four

One two
      steaming stew
Three four
      apple core
Five six
      pudding mix
Seven eight
      sugared date
Nine ten
      roasted hen
Eleven twelve
      Ukrainian cabbage rolls and pryohy

Any list of 'things' can be incorporated into a chant. In fact, a high school teacher taught us French verb forms using a chant. Words, chemical symbols, colors, and letters can all be learned by chanting them. Many different concepts can be reinforced by using the format of "One two . . . three four" or the pattern of the cheer that was used in the cherry pie chant.

Numbers in any language can find themselves in a chant. "Un deux trois", my 'franglais' chant, can be tried without worrying about language facility. The integral rhythms of the words will ease everyone into the chant. But, if the children have been in a language immersion program, they'll eat up this chant, as it combines both numbers and foods.

"One, two . . . three, four" can be done with the call-and-response technique. One or more can chant 'one, two', then one or more can respond with 'steaming stew'. Clapping can always be substituted for the numbers to vary the sound.

New lines can be added; make use of the children's creative abilities. They might suggest "thirteen, fourteen . . . jelly bean". The variations are limited only by the need to retain the rhythm of the chant.

Have everyone contribute to a list of words that rhyme with numbers. Chants can then be developed around number facts, such as:

> One plus one is two
> I love you
> Two plus two is four
> je t'adore

Let's make a salad

First you wash the lettuce
Then you spin it dry
Chop a lot of onions
till they make you cry
If you want a salad
that's the best you've had
All you have to do is
        ADD
pepper and lime
parsley and thyme
a dash of salt too
makes dressing for you
        THEN
Slice in a tomato
Add a bit of cheese
Salad in a bowl
Serve it
If you please!

The first thing to discover about this chant is the way to handle its changing rhythms. Let the children play with the lines and discover the rhythms that work best.

Then it is an easy step to watch them add the mime to accompany the words. They can wash and spin the lettuce, they can cut up the onion and cry 'Boo hoo'. They can slice the tomato and serve it around.

You could talk about why it is important to wash fruits and vegetables before eating them.

This chant could also be an opener to a discussion on what the children can do to help their families. You could end up with a scrapbook of chants based on all the helpful things they do.

Hot dogs forever

Hot dogs for breakfast
Hot dogs for lunch
Hot dogs
Hot dogs
all in a bunch

You can eat 'em with mustard
You can eat 'em with cheese
You can eat 'em
any way you please

Eat 'em from the bar-B-Q
Eat 'em from the pot
Eat 'em cold or
Eat 'em hot
Eat 'em standing up
or down on your knees

Hot dogs
Hot dogs
Please Please Please

My husband went off on a golfing holiday and I had only myself to feed. I found that there were a lot of different ways to cook hotdogs. This chant is the consequence of my solo diet.

You can do this chant very simply by just playing with the words as they are. Or you can use it as a pattern, substituting other words, such as bacon'n eggs or wieners and beans.

It might be used as a cheer. Divide the group into units of five or six. Let them be cheerleaders at a football game. They can work out a choreography to put with the words. The movement, the patterns, the dances that are devised help with children's sense of directionality, while, all the time, they are just having fun, playing with words in a rhythmical way.

Friends

Puppets are magical. They can initiate group interaction, build self-confidence, and garner responses from children who won't talk or who have difficulty talking. Puppets can be instant friends. And we know that friends are pretty magical too.

Puppet!

Puppet, can you clap
  your hands
Clap your hands
Clap your hands
Puppet, can you clap
  your hands
Clap your hands like
  this?

Oh yes, I can clap
  my hands
Clap my hands
Clap my hands
Oh yes, I can clap
  my hands
Clap my hands like
  this.

Puppet, can you
  scratch your ear
Scratch your ear
Scratch your ear
Puppet, can you
  scratch your ear
Scratch your ear like
  this?

Oh yes, I can scratch
  my ear
Scratch my ear
Scratch my ear
Oh yes, I can scratch
  my ear
Scratch my ear like
  this.

Puppet, can you bow
  down low
Bow down low
Bow down low
Puppet, can you bow
  down low
Bow down low like
  this?

Oh yes, I can bow
  down low
Bow down low
Bow down low
Oh yes, I can bow
  down low
Bow down low like
  this.

Puppet, can you
  shake your head
Shake your head
Shake your head
Puppet, can you
  shake your head
Shake your head like
  this?

Oh yes, I can shake
  my head
Shake my head
Shake my head
Oh yes,I can shake
  my head
Shake my head like
  this.

Puppet, can you
  wave good-bye
Wave good-bye
Wave good-bye
Puppet, can you
  wave good-bye
Wave good-bye like
  this?

Oh yes, I can wave
  good-bye
Wave good-bye
Wave good-bye
Oh yes, I can wave
  good-bye
Wave good-bye like
  this.

Oh yes, I can clap my hands
Scratch my ear
Bow down low
Shake my head
And wave good-bye like this.

P uppets are useful in many situations. How can something as simple as a stick puppet, made from a tongue depressor or a popsicle stick, accomplish anything? Children delight in make-believe, non-threatening puppets. Children forget any fears they might have, and join right in.

Stick puppets are easy to make; add a pie plate and you have a new personality. Cardboard tubes from paper towels make good puppets; add papier-mâché heads and they become works of art. A paper bag gives a puppet many new faces — wrinkled, squishy, puffy, or drawn-on.

One of the easiest puppets to make is a sock puppet. Pull an ordinary sock over your hand and arm with the heel on top of your hand. Start to talk to this slightly floppy 'thing' in front of the children. Find out if this 'thing' would like a mouth. A nod of agreement from your hand. Push up some of the sock into your fist; now your fingers can make the 'mouth' move. Ask the puppet if it would like eyes — one or two. If the answer is yes, have someone scrunch up a couple of pieces of masking tape and stick them onto the puppet's 'head' (that's somewhere below the heel of the sock).

The puppet is now the centre of attenion, especially as you have been having a conversation with it, not the group around. You can continue to do the talking, but the children will be watching the puppet. A good rule for a puppeteer is to keep your eyes on the puppet all the time.

A sock puppet can be made so easily that each child can make one — depending on the availability of socks — and have an instant friend.

The five simple actions that any puppet can do are given in this chant. In other words, this chant is a complete puppet workshop. The chant can be handled in several different ways. The leader of the group can have a puppet and all the children ask the puppet questions. Children can work in pairs with one or more puppets. The leader may ask questions and all the puppets can reply.

The actions used in this chant allow for independent action by the puppet. Sometimes in puppet conversation, puppets hit each other to underline a statement. This chant discourages that kind of interaction. Puppet smashing is not acceptable.

My friend

Who's the one who talks to me?
My friend.

Who's the one who walks with me?
My friend.

Who's the one who shares his pie?
My friend.

Who doesn't mind it when I cry?
My friend.

Who's always with me in the park?
My friend.

Who holds my hand when it gets dark?
My friend
My friend
My friend.

P uppets can be used to exchange lines in "My friend". The puppet that answers "My friend" can illustrate the action of the previous line as it responds.

Puppets can be used to draw out children and let them express their feelings — about people they would like as friends, people they thought were their friends, about what a good friend really is.

Hello and Goodbye

Chants have a traditional pattern. But chants need not stay within that traditional pattern. Music allows for a different kind of pattern to evolve.

Saying hello is easy

It's so easy to say hello
It's so easy to say hello
It's so easy to say hello
To say hello to you

It's so easy to shake a hand
It's so easy to shake a hand
It's so easy to shake a hand
To shake a hand with you

It's so easy to share some cake
It's so easy to share some cake
It's so easy to share some cake
To share some cake with you

It's so easy to tap a toe
It's so easy to tap a toe
It's so easy to tap a toe
To tap a toe with you

It's NOT easy to say goodbye
It's NOT easy to say goodbye
It's NOT easy to say goodbye
To say goodbye to you

It's so ea-sy to say hel-lo
It's so ea-sy to say hel-lo
It's so ea-sy to say hel-lo To
say hel-lo to you.

Some chants lend themselves to a song approach. The suggested melody may be hummed or played first but will be acquired easily by children after a few repetitions.

This is a partner chant. Each group of two can take one verse or the verses may be done in unison. The partners can act out the verses. A variation that I have tried uses three sets of partners to exchange the actions.

Additional verses are certainly possible such as, "It's so easy to wink an eye" or "It's so easy to kiss and tell". Talk about activities that are more fun to do with someone else, and the additional verses will evolve.

Group discussions can follow this chant. They might be about friends, or about families moving into a community and how those who have lived there for a while should act, or they might be about a friend or family member moving away. Such discussions might involve emotional reactions, societal responsibility, and problem-solving.

Goodbye

Goodbye
Goodbye
Goodbye
Adios
So long
Farewell
Ciao
Ta ta
and au revoir
my friend
this is
the
E
  N
    D

Good bye Good bye Good bye Adios So long Fare well
Ciao Ta Ta and au rev - oir my
friend this is the end

This chant hints at how to say goodbye in a language other than English. It can be a good way to explore how many languages are represented in any group. Chants can be used with those who have English as a second language or as a second dialect.

Drama can provide the link between linguistic and cultural environments. Ask the children, in pairs, to make a play based on a leave-taking of some sort. It need not be sad. The play could deal with a mother going to work in the morning, a friend going on a holiday, a bus driver pulling away from the bus stop. If it is appropriate, you can ask that the play reflect a particular culture. Depending on the group's size, several mini-dramas may be generated.

Remember the number chant, "Un, deux, trois"? Consider having the children write something in their native language. The discovery that there is natural rhythm in all languages will draw them into the joy of chanting, as well as breaking down any cultural barriers that may exist. Different nationalities can contribute their 'goodbye' to the existing chant. Do you have an 'auf wiedersehen', a 'sayonara', a 'dopobachynya' in the group? Once I filled a black board with phonetic spellings for all the "goodbye's" in the room.

Hallowe'en

Hallowe'en is every child's and my favorite special occasion. It combines the best of all possible elements: dressing up, make-believe, a gentle scaring, and best of all — the treats, after the tricking is over.

Here comes the witch

Here comes the witch
so don't get caught!
She'll bake you in the oven!
She'll boil you in the pot!

This chant is a perfect opener to the Hallowe'en season because it allows you to introduce the whole concept of dressing-up, the pretending to be something else. Whether working with one child or several, it is important that you dress-up in front of them. You can keep explaining that you are the same person, even though you are beginning to look quite different. You are reinforcing the concept of make-believe.

One of my most useful props is my story skirt. Mine is an easy-to-construct skirt, apron style, with several (I suggest eight) pockets. In the pockets may be bits of fabric, leather, or wool, a few wigs, a cape, a book, puppets—anything that I can use to add visual effects as I introduce a chant. I sometimes call my story skirt my 'table of contents' because I can design a story that leads into a chant by reaching into one of my pockets and producing a new 'object'. Children watch in fascination as object after object is pulled out of this pocket or that. Instructions for making a story skirt are on page 106.

Most children enjoy being gently scared in make-believe play, especially at Hallowe'en. Witch, ghost, and goblin poems are delightful if they are introduced properly.

A story skirt or a grab-bag of any sort can produce a witch. A big, black wig, a pointed hat, a cape or a gown — and you *are* a witch. As soon as the children know that you are a witch, you can play games in role as a witch.

Blindfold yourself and place yourself in the centre of a circle of children. The children march or dance around you, chanting "Here comes the witch." When a player is touched by the witch, he or she is 'it'. The simple chant will come very easily to the players.

Ask the children to tell you everything they know about witches. Write it all down.

Boil the bats

Boil the bats
Stir in rats
snakes and scales
slippery tails
and here's for you
a witch's brew!

N ow that you are the witch, do what witches do best: make a witches' brew. The process of stirring up a dreadful concoction can be mimed by the children. Players can add their own ingredients — spiders, slugs, a vegetable they hate, are possibilities. Players can circle the imaginary cauldron, throwing in new ingredients and chanting. If you have carved some pumpkins, light them, turn off other lights, and create an even better environment for brew-making.

Hallowe'en parade

Witches, goblins, skeletons, ghosts,
Tell us the costume you love most.

Black cat
Fat cat
Hissing at the moon
Black cat
Scary cat
Riding on a broom

Black cat
Fat bat
Spider toad
Hallowe'en parade
Comin' down the road

A child's imagination has no bounds when it is costume time. Any parent with a malfunctioning sewing machine (intentional or not) will attest to the level of imagination. Children can see themselves as many other people, characters, and things. It is a time for magical moments, despite the moment when imagination crashes into the practicality of what *can* be produced as a costume.

You may have dressed up as a witch, but now it is everyone else's turn. Chant "Hallowe'en parade" in unison and then add a description of the costumes you see around you. Costumes are to be shared: their originality, their concept, their handiwork. Everyone should share in this parade of make-believe.

As the parade of costumed children proceeds, the chanting voices may change. The chanters can shriek like monsters, whisper because they are frightened or subdued, and even use a witch's voice, shrill and dissonant. The costumes will suggest other appropiate voices.

Hallowe'en

Hallowe'en
Spooky scene
Witches mean
Gremlins green
Skel'tons lean
Magic bean
Goblins keen
Ghosties clean
Often seen
    on
Hallowe'en
Hallowe'en
Hallowe'eee
          e
         e
       e
        e
         e
          e
         e
          e
         e
          n!

Spooks

Hallowe'en is the time for you
for stories, songs, and magic brew
for poems of goblins
and chants of cats
for casting spells in pointed hats

These chants can be used to introduce Hallowe'en costumes too. The children can move around the room in a circle, changing their voices for each line.

A witch's voice is a logical one but so are bellows, whispers, shouts, yells, and singing. Every group with which I have chanted "Hallowe'en" has found that a spooky screech is the appropriate ending.

Let the children draw themselves in costume — crayon resist or scratch pictures might be a good medium. Or have the children lie on a big piece of paper on the floor; they can trace each other's bodies. Then everyone can fill in his or her costume.

Hauntin' blues

If you wanna go a-hauntin'
Let me tell you what to do
Get a pot of witch's brew
Make a spell in the middle of the night
Fly through the sky and give 'em a fright
Fly spooky
Gobble-de-gooky

T alking blues or rapping have been a part of our speech pattern for a long time. Let the children discover which words they want to accent to vary the rhythm of the chant. There is a tradition of movement associated with talking blues — thigh-slapping, finger-snapping, shoulder-shrugging, sometimes, today, breakdancing accompanies the "rapster" on the streets of cities like Philadelphia, New York, and Toronto.

Everyone can stand for this talking blues chant. The beat can be emphasized by snapping fingers. Two lines of players can move in opposite directions, to the beat. Particular actions will be discovered. I always let children move in their own way, trying for casual movement that is not too regimented. They may sway, step forward and back, crouch down, slide, move on tip-toe, or jump up. Some real breakdancers may surface!

A chant like "Hauntin' blues" with its integral movement possibilities improves the co-ordination of any children who need help, and everyone will enjoy the movements. Body awareness and control are important learning experiences.

Dance of the bones

old bones rattling
yellow teeth snapping
bald head wagging
arms flip flopping
long legs clicking
knee bones knocking
skipping prancing
'round the room
'round and 'round and 'round the room

crickety crack
down and back
bones hopping
bones dropping
pieces popping
'round the room
'round and 'round and 'round the room

S tories and poems can inspire chants. This chant developed after I read a story by Alvin Schwartz. The description of a skeleton's dance produced a lively image for me. The chant can be used after telling Schwartz's story, another of a similar nature, or can stand on its own macabre merit. Good background music could be the "Danse Macabre". Children will devise movements that suit the words. Try accelerating the speed of the chant, faster, faster, faster until the bones drop. Add music which could be one note, or one minor chord to this chant.

One group of children might enjoy creating a dance drama to illustrate the chant. They could show their dance drama while the others chant in the background. A tableau or frozen picture could be made for part of the chant while others chant the words.

Alvin Schwartz listened to a group of librarians chanting "Dance of the bones" and commented, "The tales sound better than ever with your interpretation."

Trick or treating

Trick or treating!
Trick or treating!
Everybody come around.
Trick or treating!
Trick or treating!

Let's eat yummies
by the pound

caramel kisses
rosy apples
colored smarties
jellied jujubes
buttered popcorn
sticky licorice
chocolate cookies
peanut brittle
sour lemon
gooey gum drops
soft marshmallows

Oh my tummy!
Indigestion!
Alka Seltzer!
Call the doctor!

D ressing up for Hallowe'en leads to trick or treating or shelling out. This chant lets everyone add his or her favorite treats. Start by chanting in unison. The basic tempo of dah, dah, dee, dah will be picked up by the children. They can add their own treats following the same tempo — use 'rosy apples' with its four beats, as the example of the tempo. Another chant that uses the same measure and also allows for personal addition is:

> Witch's cauldron
> Witch's cauldron
> Everybody slink along

> Witch's cauldron
> Witch's cauldron
> Witches soon will come to town

> hairy spiders
> toasted lizards
> ugly toenails
> slimy eyeballs . . .

This chant can also be used as a model for other co-operative chants. For example:

> Christmas dinner
> Christmas dinner
> Everybody gather 'round
> Christmas dinner
> Christmas dinner
> eating turkey
> by the pound

> mashed potatoes
> buttered carrots
> giblet dressing . . .

Ask the children to suggest other special occasions, especially those that centre around food. The customs of several may be introduced by the children. Drawings could show each child's family when gathered together for a special occasion.

Special Occasions

Everyone has a favorite special occasion; I've already admitted that mine is Hallowe'en. The following chants talk about two more — Valentine's Day and birthdays.

Valentine, Valentine

Give me
Give me
Give me
Give me your love.

Never
Never
Never
Give me a shove.

Give me
Give me
Give me
Give me your pop

Never
Never
Never
Give me a chop.

Give me
Give me
Give me
Give me a sign

That you'll always be my
Valentine!

This chant can be done in unison, but I often divide the group so that a two part round can develop. I start very simply by asking them to do alternate verses. Then the first and second verses can be chanted simultaneously, then the third and fourth verses. Everyone chants the final verse. Or several can begin the chant and others join in with the first line when the second line is reached and so on — a staggered entry into the chant changes the overall tone of the chant.

Puppets could "speak" alternating verses as an opener to the participation of the children.

I love you

the heart of the matter
still remains
when you're not around
it always rains

some rain I love
but some feels bad
when you're not around
I'm always sad

S imple actions can be added to this chant. In a larger group, give some the chant to say, others the actions to do, and ask the rest to reinforce the beat with a drum or other available instrument. Thigh-slapping and quiet clapping can also be used to heighten the beat.

A chant like this with simple actions can be used if children are asked to "perform" for their parents.

Whose birthday is it?

Is this the birthday party?
Uh Huh
Is this the birthday party?
Uh Huh
Is everybody here?
Uh Huh
Is Andy here?
Uh Huh
Is Brian here?
Uh Huh
Is Carol here?
Uh Huh
Is Deborah here?
Uh Huh
Is Ellen here?
Uh Huh
Is Francis here?
Uh Huh
Is Gordie here?
Uh Huh
Is Heidi here?
Uh Huh
Is Ivan here?
Uh Huh
Is Jimmy here?
Uh Huh
Is Kevin here?
Uh Huh
Is Lisa here?
Uh Huh

Is Marty here?
  Uh Huh
Is Nadine here?
  Uh Huh
Is Oryst here?
  Uh Huh
Is Penny here?
  Uh Huh
Is Quentin here?
  Uh Huh
Is Ronnie here?
  Uh Huh
Is Sonja here?
  Uh Huh
Is Tommy here?
  Uh Huh
Is Una here?
  Uh Huh
Is Vera here?
  Uh Huh
Is Willie here?
  Uh Huh
Is Yuri here?
  Uh Huh
Is Zenon here?
  Uh Huh
WHOSE BIRTHDAY IS IT?   Kevin's
HAPPY BIRTHDAY KEVIN!   Thank You.
Is everybody hungry?
  Uh Huh!
  LET'S EAT!

Each letter of the alphabet is used in this call-and-response chant. But every group can substitute its own names without worrying about covering the alphabet from A to Z.

If the group is in a circle, the person named can hop into the centre of the circle. I have found that some children, particularly boys, cannot figure out how to sidestep while moving around in a circle. I tell them to stop a puck; they can all do that! Then I suggest they stop the puck in goal five times, moving in the same direction. They are side-stepping in no time.

I won't

I won't take this cod liver oil
I won't eat those carrots I hate
I won't wash my hands
I won't comb my hair
I won't go to bed before eight
I won't put the cap on the toothpaste
Mom, what did you say? I can't hear

Well, carrots aren't bad.
Where is my comb, Dad?
Did you say my birthday is near?

This chant is about a birthday too, but it allows children to name all the things they hate doing.

Since birthdays are special occasions, make a ''special occasion'' surprise such as a Mexican *pinata* from either tissue paper or papier-mâché.

Geography

Playing with the names of places is delightful. We have so many rhythmical, silly, interesting place names. Geography acquires a whole new dimension when sound poems are developed about places.

Our country

Canada Canada
miles and miles wide
five thousand kilometres
side to side
ten fine provinces
all in a row
cities by the hundreds
places to go
coast to coast
towns galore
from B.C. to Labrador
rivers, mountains, prairies too
five great lakes
and all for you!

A great opener for any geography lesson on Canada, this chant has varied rhythmical patterns within it. Let the children work with the words until they find a pattern that feels comfortable to them.

Ask the children to write a patriotic cheer for their town or city.

Labrador is just a bowl of berries

Labrador flora
Labrador tea
Cloudberry
Blackberry
Crowberry

Crackerberry
Squashberry
Bunchberry too

Mix 'em all together
for Labrador brew

On a visit to Labrador, I received a package of hasti-notes as an appreciation gift for my presentation of chants. Admiring them on the flight home, I realized that each note illustrated a different Labrador berry. This is the found poem that happened as I shuffled through my gift.

Using this chant as a model, I try to develop a chant with the children that relates to their particular town or region. I ask the children to name things that they associate with where they live. Usually, several categories are given and then we work on the chant. Crops can be a good category; for example, the varieties of grapes found in the Niagara or Calonna regions. Types of businesses that are found close-by or types of vehicles that are commonplace can also lead to descriptions in chant-form of their particular environment.

Is this a choo choo train?

Choo Choo
Choo Choo

choo choo train
choo choo train

Is this the choo choo train?
 Yes, Man!
Is this the choo choo train?
 Yes, Man!

Is it going to Ayr?
 Yes, Man!
Is it going to Birr?
 Yes, Man!
Is it going to Carp?
 Yes, Man!
Is it going to Doon?
 Yes, Man!
Is it going to Epps?
 Yes, Man!
Is it going to Finch?
 Yes, Man!
Is it going to Galt?
 Yes, Man!
Is it going to Holt?
 Yes, Man!
Is it going to Keene?
 Yes, Man!
Is it going to Leith?
 Yes, Man!

Is it going to Muir?
        Yes, Man!
Is it going to Nairn?
        Yes, Man!
Is it going to Orf?
        Yes, Man!
Is it going to Puce?
        Yes, Man!
Is it going to Queen's?
        Yes, Man!
Is it going to Read?
        Yes, Man!
Is it going to Spence?
        Yes, Man!
Is it going to Troy?
        Yes, Man!
Is it going to Ulch?
        Yes, Man!
Is it going to Vars?
        Yes, Man!
Is it going to Wye?
        Yes, Man!
Is it going to Xavier?
        Yes, Man!
Is it going to York?
        Yes, Man!
Is it going to Zor?
        Yes, Man!
Are you getting on?
        Yes, Man!

ALL ABOARD !

W hat a natural way to build a train! Children can hook onto the engine with the introduction of each town. Each child can choose a town to represent. The towns can be the ones in the chant or ones that the children suggest.

The whole group can chant the introduction. Then one-half can ask the question, after which the other half shouts "Yes, Man!" or "Okay" while the child whose town has been given in the question hooks onto the train.

As the train becomes longer and longer, it can begin to move around the space. Different movements can be suggested for the train such as hopping, skipping, shuffling, and wiggling.

If the children must stay seated, this chant can be done as a call-and-response. The delight in using place names they know will stimulate any group. You can try variations such as "Is this the aer-o-plane? Is it going to France? . . ."

The Ontariodrog

The Ontariodrog is a monster
huge in the harbor of Toronto
It drinks the water for its grog
and eats up small kids pronto.

After chanting this nonsense poem, I ask the children to make up names of monsters that might live in their town, their province, in a body of water that is near them, or in a garbage dump.

I then have everyone write a chant about this monster, and then make a drawing of the monster. The extension into art continues to develop descriptive and expressive language. Rather than drawing their monsters, they could sculpt them from a flour and water paste with strips of newspaper. Or scraps of wood can be used as the vehicle to describe their imaginary creatures. Marvellous monsters can be structured from scraps of any sort: leather, wool, wire, string, cardboard, foil. But, best of all, children might construct their monsters from the most concrete medium of all — their own bodies. They can then present a tableau of monsters and make them "come alive".

Now that the monsters have physical characteristics, ask the children to create a chant for what a monster might say. For example:

Awk, grr, grock, grack,
I'm as a tall as a super stack.

Weather

What does everyone talk about? The weather. And we can chant about it too: an easy and fun way to introduce some science lessons.

Raindrops in my shoes

Raindrops in my shoes
Raindrops in my shoes
Sloshy slushy
Sloshy slushy
Raindrops in my shoes

Snowflakes on my nose
Snowflakes on my nose
Sniffle snuffle
Sniffle snuffle
Snowflakes on my nose

Cookies on my plate
Cookies on my plate
Gobble grobble
Gobble grobble
Cookies on my plate

C hildren can design the actions to accompany this chant. Let them walk with raindrops in their shoes — there will be as many illustrations of this as there are people in the group. Now catch snowflakes on your nose — I bet tongues will be part of the catching! The cookies can be gobbled by different personae: gobble them like a giant, nibble them like a mouse, swallow them like a wolf.

The alliteration and repetition of words establishes the beat but it can be reinforced by patsch (thigh slapping) or by using instruments.

Rain

listen listen
listen to the rain
listen listen
listen to the rain
listen listen listen listen
listen to the rain.

softer softer
listen to the rain
softer softer
listen to the rain
listen listen listen listen
listen to the rain

louder louder
listen to the rain
louder louder
listen to the rain
listen listen listen listen
listen to the rain

The repetition of words helps the rhythm of this one, and mimics the sound of rain. I talk about rain and how there are several different kinds of rain. It can be gentle, it can be clattering against the window, it can have a lot of wind with it, it can be cold.

The second verse suggests a gentle spring rain. The third verse is about a harsh fall rain. These verses can begin in a normal voice and change in level during the verse. By the end the voices are either whispering or shouting. Rubbing the palms of your hands together makes the sound of gentle rain.

The boats to Bequia

roll on
roll off
the *Grenadine Star*

roll on
roll off
you can go far

roll on
roll off
the *Friendship Rose*

roll on
roll off
sailing she goes

roll on
roll off Bequia Isle

roll on
roll off
the people all smile

Most Canadians love the warmth of southern islands. I am no exception. On a trip south, we had to take the mail boat from St. Vincent to the island of Bequia. The boat couldn't quite come into the shore so a gangplank was dropped into the water offshore. We had to wade through the water, holding aloft our luggage, clamber onto the shaky plank, and roll onto the boat. The mail boat also carried goats, so it was a pretty funny scene as we all rolled onto the boat amidst animals, luggage, and local residents. This chant is the result of that visit to a warmer climate. The chant has a musical sense which could be enhanced be adding simple music.

The World of Work

Children know a lot about the world of work — more than they may realize. They watch work being done on the roads as they walk to school; they know that someone 'special' often needs to be called if the oven stops working or the water pipes start to drip. Members of their family go to work as do their next-door neighbors.

Helping

All the people in our town
help to make the world go 'round

Judge
Professor
Hair dresser

Cook
Hatter
Baseball batter

Priest
Musician
Obstetrician

Nurse
Lawyer
Bug destroyer

Dentist
Writer
Fire fighter

These are only but a few
See if you can rhyme some too.

K ids love this chant — they can share their knowledge of various jobs and make rhyming couplets for them.   You could introduce a discussion on work by letting the children mime certain jobs and see if the others can guess what the job is. Think of farmers, firefighters, truck drivers, nurses, typists, rock singers, ballet dancers, surgeons.

Different objects can also be shown and guesses made about who would use what in what job. A saucepan can be shown (for chef, mother, father), a shovel (for gardener, construction worker, farmer), a thermometer (for nurse, doctor, parents, babysitters), a book (for teacher, librarian, student), balls (for baseball, football, soccer players), a plane (for pilot, flight attendant, business traveller). How about a flashlight, a clock, or a plant from the garden? Guessing games involve everyone and so build self-confidence. These particular guessing games also help improve the important skill of classifying.

Children might use still pictures or statues of themselves in various jobs. The tableau would become animated as each child showed his or her line of work.

Teachers

Teachers do this
and teachers do that
and teachers pull rabbits
out of a hat.

Teachers sing songs
and teachers are good
teachers play dress-up
in cape and hood.

Teachers mark papers
teachers tie boots
listen to screaming
hollers and hoots.

One specific job is given here. In a classroom or playground situation, I have asked kids to add tasks they think a teacher does; I'm always surprised with their perceptions.

Other particular jobs can be fitted into this pattern — what about a vet, a gas station worker (either a mechanic or a gas-pumper), a grocery store clerk?

The firefighter

Who's the bravest man about
the one who puts the fires out
the one who climbs the ladders tall
and rescues kittens from the wall?

Put down those matches!
Drop that lighter!
Don't make work for
the FIREFIGHTER!

This chant also talks about a specific job and can be used to highlight a visit to a firehall. Or invite a firefighter to visit you, bringing along some of his "stuff". Safety posters that relate to the causes of fires can be an adjunct to this chant. You might ask the children to draw what they think a firefighter does. Discussion will produce the fact that most jobs involve quite a few different tasks. For instance, a firefighter does fight fires but he or she also rescues animals in distress, talks to people about safety, practises first aid, and inspects buildings to make sure they are safe.

Doctor, doctor

Doctor, doctor
get here quick
My cabbage patch dolly
is sick, sick, sick
She's got the sniffles
She's got the flu
She's even got
the doodle de doo.
I gave her syrup
and chicken soup
and now she's come down
with the croup
So, doctor please
don't mind the weather
Come right now
and make her better.

A sk the children what movements are suggested to them by the rhythm or words of this chant. Let them experiment with various movements until they find ones that seem to work best.

I often add visual effects when working with this chant such as dolls, stuffed toys, and puppets.

Use some of the jobs that were suggested from chanting "Helping" and let the children make up new chants. There is great joy in creating something that is uniquely theirs, whether done individually or in groups. I then cover the walls with the new chants that have been created.

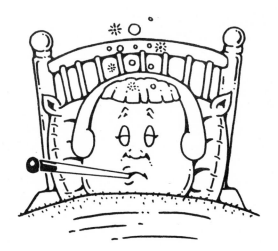

Building

Bulldozer
Jackhammer
Cement truck

Crushing rocks
Moving muck

Riveter
Grader
Hot steam drill

Building a city
for Bonnie and Bill

I ntroduce a discussion of environment with this chart. In most communities, buildings are going up and coming down. A skyscraper or a barn may be under construction; a new housing subdivision may be close by; a building is being demolished. All construction produces noises and confusion, often mud, and sometimes traffic congestion. And construction always produces something new, exciting, and different.

The children can produce a street map of their community. The finished product can be as complex or as simple as the age level warrants. Several children can work together on the project. The co-operation required and the decisions that will need to be made will reinforce those particular skills. Models of houses, stores, trees, etc. can be added. Materials used will again depend on the age of the builders. Playdough, plasticine, and papier-mâché are all possibilities.

Extensions from this building project can be the acquiring of new language — to label the parts of the street map properly; mathematical skills — from trying to estimate how far "this is from that"; cross-cultural awareness — particularly if several neighborhoods are depicted; and a knowledge of the environmental conditions in their neighborhood.

There are many different workers involved in building, and most of them have a particular sound associated with their work: a carpenter hitting nails with a hammer, a driller breaking up concrete, a dump truck driver backing up. Make a tape of some of these construction noises. The discovery of how many of these sounds they recognize will have a positive effect on the children.

Learning to listen, and then learning auditory discrimination, are important activities. Auditory awareness develops through an exposure to singing games, action responses, and sound puzzles, according to one curriculum guide. Chants can fit all three descriptions — perfect 'jump-offs' for auditory awareness.

Space Travel

No matter how many shuttles and satellites have been sent into orbit, space travel remains fascinating. Naïve or sophisticated, we all have thoughts of what it might be like — if we went.

Would you still come home?

Would you fly to the moon
if you had the chance?
Would you jump in a space suit
and try to dance?

If you had lots of cash
and you had lots of time,
would you ride to Mars
on a silver dime?

Would you jet to Venus
on a flying ship,
and head to Neptune
for the next eclipse?

But would you still come home
for fish and chips?

I think this is a dynamite chant — and most kids agree with me. It is a whimsical look at space travel that catches their imaginations.

Let them enjoy chanting it in unison. Some of them may want to illustrate the words of the chant.

McSpace

McMoon
McVenus
McMars
A hamburger stand in the stars
Fly into McSpace and
fill your McFace and
take a McSwing
on McStars

Driving home from an out-of-town visit, we were commenting on the number of fast food franchises. This led to thinking about what would happen if space were opened up to commercial outlets.

Chant in unison, just for the pleasure of hearing the words. Have fun inventing new words with 'Mc' as a prefix. Build words around other prefixes, such as sub.

A short commercial might be written that would try to sell McShoes, or McCombs, or McToothbrushes.

Stars on Mars

Are there stars on Mars?
Do they play guitars?
Do they eat nut bars
and mints in jars?
Do they drive big cars
or minotaurs?
Can they make big scars
with scimitars?
These stars on Mars.
These stars on Mars.

Another nonsense chant about space that can be enjoyed for its pure silliness. Or it can be extended into art or into dance. Children can use scarves, ribbons, silk squares to make a dance sequence in which movements are changed according to the phrasing of the chant.

Flying

Would you go into orbit
if you were invited
on a silver shuttle
with lunch provided?

Would you guzzle a malted
from the milky pathway
and not phone your mother
for the whole long day?

Would you fly to Saturn?
Would you streak to Mars?
Then would you jet back home
on the shooting stars?

This nonsense chant could be used as a springboard for a discussion of what we know about other planets and such phenomena as shooting stars. Or children can write a short story that describes what they imagine they might do if they had a chance to "go into orbit".

Noah and His Ark

Thousands of stories have been written about Noah and the ark.
Here is another one.

Noah and his ark

The animals were crowded
and the rain
wouldn't stop
They were jammed
up like traffic
but there was
no cop
They jiggled and
they wiggled
in the dismal dark
Oops!Oh lordy
trouble started
in the ark

Bee stung bear
who was rocking in her chair

Bear growled at mouse
through the hole to her house

Mouse squeaked at frog
who was trying to jog

Frog croaked at pig
in her brand new wig

Pig squealed at cat
with his tall silk hat

Cat meowed at snake
who was just awake

Snake hissed at cow
who said, "Yikes it's a row"

Cow mooed at dog
as he peered through the fog

Dog barked at fox
who was darning his sox

Fox snarled at lion
And lion
went cryin'
in his big gold boa
straight to Noah

"Whoa!" shouted Noah
"This noise is too big!"
When along flew a dove
with an olive twig

"Dear," said his missus
"Isn't this grand?
Look out there
at all of that land.
The rain has stopped;
Let's all get out."
The animals cheered
and began to shout,
"We're quite ready
to disembark.
Thank you Noah
for the ride
on your ark!"

The sun came out,
a rainbow shone;
It only took a minute
and the animals were gone

"Whew" sighed Noah.
"They nearly caused a riot."

His wife made tea
and they drank it
in the quiet.

This chant can be tackled in several ways depending on the size of the group. The first verse can be said in unison; then individuals can take two lines each, working through the animals. Noah and his wife then have parts until the unison chanting of "We're quite ready to disembark . . ."

The different sounds made by the animals can be heightened by imitative sounds or by actions. If the group is large enough this aspect can be taken by non-chanters.

Children will discover that they can change some sounds. For instance, the chanters can growl the word "growl" and make it quite elongated. Or they may change "Whoa!" shouted Noah to "Wo — ah" shouted Noah!

The last three lines can be chanted very softly as a contrast to all the activity in the previous lines.

The separate images of the chant may be illustrated and put together as a "roller show". For instance, ask several children to illustrate the introductory scene on the ark; then one can draw the bear rocking in its chair being stung by the bee; another can draw the bear growling at the mouse that is peeking out of its house, and so on.

All the drawings can be assembled in sequence and fastened together. A theatre can be made by cutting away the front of a big cardboard box. Cut two holes in each side of the box. The beginning and end drawings are attached to broom handles, and all the intervening drawings rolled on. Then the story of the chant can be 'rolled' from beginning to end.

While the story is being shown, the chant can be read in unison or by individuals taking roles. Such a show could become a travelling show, one to be shared with other groups. Many skills come together in one enjoyable experience — and all because of that Noah and his ark.

Miscellany

There were some chants that would not fit into the pattern of the book, but were special enough to be included in the collection.

Singing sand

We are the dunes of singing sand
singing
singing
songs sung low
songs of caravans
songs of camel bells
We are the dunes of singing sand
singing
singing
silken songs
songs of quartz on wings of wind
singing
singing
our desert song.

Did you know that Soviet scientists have discovered dunes of singing sand in the central Asian Karakum Desert? When a gust of wind sweeps over the dunes, myriads of dry sand grains begin to make a low singing sound. Scientists say that the sound is generated as electrical charges are set up on the surface of quartz grains when they are moved by the wind. I wrote the chant after I heard about this amazing natural phenomenon.

The gentle, singing quality of the words will suggest a musical chant. The reason for my writing the chant could be an interesting lead-in to a science lesson.

Condo kid

In our condominium
down goes the garbage
up goes the elevator
over goes the airplane
under goes the motor car
between goes the balcony
through goes the pussy cat
around goes the rainstorm
out goes the puppy dog
and
In Goes Me!

I am the condo kid in this chant, but it can relate to anyone who lives in an apartment building. They will understand all the events that are introduced by the prepositions.

This chant can lead into a discussion of other types of homes. What about camper vans, cottages, houses, tents? Simple box models of various housing alternatives can be made by the children. Bungalows, townhouses, duplexes, apartments can all be constructed. The box models could even lead to new chants about how life goes on in the different configurations.

The blanket doesn't feel right

I heard a noise in the basement
It gave me quite a fright!
And I don't want to go to bed now,
'cause the blanket doesn't feel right.

On a scary night, on a scary night
the blanket doesn't feel right!

I saw a creepy shadow
It was a spooky sight!
And I don't want to go to bed now
'cause the blanket doesn't feel right.

On a scary night, on a scary night
the blanket doesn't feel right!

There's someone in the attic
it's dark and there's no light!
And I don't want to go to bed now,
'cause the blanket doesn't feel right.

On a scary night, on a scary night
the blanket doesn't feel right!

I t had been a typical Hallowe'en — the fun of dresing-up, the thrill of going from house to house, the treats before bed. Our children were now ready for bed. But, my younger son, Kevin, said: "The blanket doesn't feel right". With all of its delights, Hallowe'en still had its scary side; the witches and goblins were still around. Kevin's concerns authored this chant.

Kids do have fears, particularly of the noises heard in their homes. Sometimes these fears occur at night when they are alone in their bedroom; sometimes these fears happen when they go home after school and no one else is there.

Let the children talk about how they feel in their homes when they are on their own. The sharing of experiences will help.

If you want, you can read the children some poems about being afraid to increase their knowledge that everyone has such feelings at times.

I'm glad I'm adopted
For Todd and Tara

Adopted, adopted,
I'm glad I am adopted
because my mother said
"We picked you 'cause we wanted you
we loved your tiny head;
And when we took a look at you
your eyes shone like the sun
it didn't take a second
to know YOU were the one!"

You will recognize the times when using this chant would be appropriate. It need not be just because you know that someone in the group has been adopted. It is a good conversation-opener to talk about families, adoptions, and differences in attitude.

Little black fly

If you get bitten
by a little black fly
If a little black fly
bites your little blue eye

Go to the medicine chest
And lift the latch

Get yourself a little eye patch

Little black fly
Little black fly
Why'd ya have to bite me on my eye?

T his chant in honor of every cottager's arch enemy seemed an appropriate ending. A chant *can* be devised about anything — fun things, sad things, everyday occurrences. And a chant can be done by anyone.

A chant can also be devised quickly. The following simple chant happened in two seconds as I was driving along an expressway. The name of a town on a signpost made me laugh and made me say: Innerkip Drumbo
Chicken gumbo
Mumbo jumbo
Alcan bumbo

Chants are another way of talking about things — but in that 'other way' you can change voices, change tempo, alter moods, be someone else, learn something — quite a lot to gain from a simple chant and all while you are having fun!

Making a Story Skirt

Following these directions will give you a story skirt that can be your table of contents for many storytelling sessions.

Materials: 3 m denim, 115 cm wide
2 m print material, 115 cm wide
piece of flannel, 35 cm × 40 cm
piece of lightweight wood, 25 cm × 30 cm

Cut one metre from the denim. The remaining two metres are the main part of your apron-style story skirt. Taking into account that a 20 cm ruffle is to be added, cut the denim to the right length for you.

Cut the print material as follows:

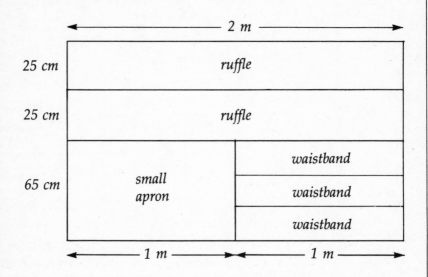

Join together the two pieces 2 m × 25 cm to make the ruffle. Hem. Run two rows of basting stitch the length of the ruffle. Gather to about half of its length, and stitch to the bottom of the skirt. Hem each side of the denim/print.

The piece of print 65 cm × 1 m will become a smaller apron on the front of the skirt. The piece of flannel will be on the underside of this apron, and will provide an envelope for the wood. When you are seated, the lapboard will provide a performance stage or be a flannel board when flipped up.

First run a zig zag stitch on all four sides of the flannel. Fold the piece of print in half and press the fold line. Unfold, and stitch the flannel to the right side of the print at the fold line. Stitch three sides; one side is left open for the wood. Fold the print in half again with right sides together. Stitch both long sides. Turn right side out. Stitch the top of the print to the centre top of the denim, keeping the flannel next to the denim.

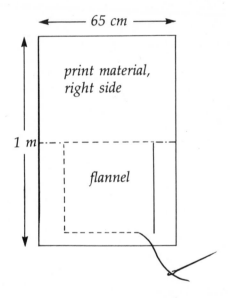

From the remaining metre of denim cut nine pieces about 30 cm × 38 cm to make the pockets. Hem one long side of each piece which will be the top. Sew the other three sides, with a zig zag stitch, onto the appropriate places on your skirt.

Run two rows of basting stitch along the top of the skirt with its attached print apron. Gather to your waist size.

Sew together the three pieces of print 20 cm × 1 m to make the waistband with ties. With the right side of the print and the right side of the denim together, centre the waistband on the skirt. Stitch the length of the skirt's waist. Turn the skirt and its attached waistband over. Press along the length of the waistband. Fold the waistband over one-third, and then over one-third again to join with the skirt. Stitch the length of the waistband, catching the skirt. Hem the ends of the ties.

Now you can slide the wood into its flannel sleeve and fill the pockets.

If you do not want to sew your own story skirt, use a carpenter's apron.

Some of the same effects can be achieved with a story hat.

Take any favorite hat, straw or felt, and suspend small articles from its brim, using fishing line. Each article can represent a story. For instance, a small skull could be a fairly traditional entry to "Dance of the bones". Artificial food could introduce "Junk food" or "Let's make a salad". Bits of fabric could introduce the concept of dressing-up for any of the Hallowe'en chants. A frog, a lion, or a mouse could begin "Noah and his ark".

Obviously, the articles have to be lightweight, but they can be changed to suit the topic. The hat becomes a table of contents for the person wearing it, just as the story skirt does.

Index